Chocolate Toothpaste
&
Christmas Cheer

KIM LUKE

Chocolate Toothpaste and Christmas Cheer
The Enchanted Farm at Fort Osage
Third Tale in the Series

For information:

kimjluke59@gmail.com or www.kimlukeauthor.com

Illustrations by rembrandtsister.com

Published in the United States by Personal Chapters LLC

ISBN-13: 978-1979988032
ISBN-10: 197998803X

Other Books by Kim Luke
Circle of Sun
Black Inferno
Mortal Moon
The King of Nobody Finds His Castle
Builders, Bakers & Fairy Tale Makers

All the mystery and magic of Christmas is seen through the eyes of every child who visits Fort Osage Farm. Their innocence and wonder touch my heart and inspire me. This book is for them all.

Special thanks to my editor, Anne Tezon and Personal Chapters LLC, and to my illustrator, Rembrandt's Sister.

To Jackson,
   Be brave, be like Ollie!
              Kim Luke

Chapter 1

Gypsy the cat soaks up warmth from the afternoon fire in the living room at Fort Osage Farm. Farmer Bob and Honey are enjoying football on television wearing their warm slippers and snuggling under cozy blankets.

"The weather man is predicting snow, and lots of it." the famer tells his wife with a sigh. "This might be the most snow we've seen in a long time."

"That will make it difficult for the families coming out to our farm to choose their Christmas trees." Honey replies with concern.

"It may ruin our first-ever Christmas show in our new lodge," Farmer Bob adds, shaking his head.

Karibou, the fluffy white Alaskan Malamute, can't take the heat anymore. He squirms and fidgets before going straight to the door. Honey lets him out.

Karibou breathes in the brisk air, glad to be outdoors. His steps crunch the dry leaves that lie over the brown grass on his way to the dock. He plops down and rests his head on his paws, perfectly comfortable in his winter coat. He was made for this kind of weather.

Summer has given way to the crisp red, golden ambers and warm rusts of autumn. The distant honking of geese overhead grabs his attention as they fly south to warmer places.

"Hello Karibou," the garden snake Ugo says from the pond's edge.

"Hi Ugo! How are you this fine day?"

"It is time to go underground and escape winter's cold. I can't survive without going deep into the mud at the bottom of Lily Pad Pond. There I will stay until the warm weather returns."

"Goodbye for now, until spring then?" Karibou asks.

"Yes, I'm afraid so. Would you care to join me? I don't feel we've bonded as friends. We have so much in common; both the heroic type and all."

Karibou doesn't follow what Ugo means.

"I don't live in the mud in the winter months. I was made for weather like this. I'm at my best when the wind blows and the snow is flying."

"How nice for you," Ugo responds before sighing. "Every year I make a wish to the great Mother Nature to transform me into something majestic like you, so that come spring I am changed. But, sadly my wishes are not granted."

"I don't think we can change in that way," Karibou says. "And why would you want to Ugo? You are a snake and a fine one at that."

"Your words are kind, but everyone is still afraid of me."

"It is more important what you think of yourself."

"You are wise, Karibou," Ugo admits.

"I learned that from Ollie. He knew what he wanted and had to ignore what others were saying. And now he is king of his own castle."

"I think you are on to something! I will spend my months waiting with a new attitude."

"That's the spirit, my friend. See you in the spring!"

Later in the day, snowflakes fall from the gray skies, some landing on Karibou's nose. He lazily watches the snow quickly cover the ground.

Fenwick trots around the far side of the pond, his reddish coat standing out against the white scene. Karibou goes to him.

"Hi friend," Karibou announces. Fenwick smiles and turns.

"Hello Karibou, Your winter coat matches the snow. You are almost invisible!"

"Yes, I love the snow. I am an Alaskan dog breed, and snow is my favorite thing. You look different Fenwick."

"My undercoat gives me extra warmth and size. And now that the rats are gone, there's plenty to eat, so I've added a few pounds. I'm busy now preparing for the storm."

"Farmer Bob talks of the storm. What will you do?"

"I don't mind the snow. My den is dry and my coat keeps me comfortable. But the blowing snow is different, so I am gathering extra food, and I must finish right away. The storm is coming. Good bye friend!"

Karibou trots over the white grounds, up to the loft and repeats the words "mini me."

Now that he is small, he can tell Ollie the news. Winter has come to Fort Osage Farm.

Chapter 2

Ollie opens his eyes to his palace home, almost forgetting he is now king of his own castle. Right away his heart skips a beat. He closes his eyes for a little pep talk.

"It's normal to be afraid of new things. I shall rule with faith and courage. I am now a king, and the kingdom needs me." His words get his day started on the right foot.

Ollie draws a blanket around his shoulders to stay warm on this bitter cold morning. He adds a log to the fire and then another. The flames leap around the fresh logs and Ollie warms up. With his blanket around his shoulders he poses in the mirror.

He stands taller, pretending he is wearing royal robes. He lifts his chin and puffs his chest out.

"Good morning to all my subjects. How are you all this fine day? Today we will . . ."

Ollie's shoulders drop as he searches for words. He clears his throat and tries again. "Today is the day . . ." again he stops.

Ollie is unsure what he should say or do. He wanted to be a king, but now he feels lost. Like a ship without sails. Ollie wanders around his room. He places his foot on the hearth and strikes a royal pose, but his new role just feels like a scratchy sweater.

Ollie does not like this feeling. He paces around the room.

"A breath of fresh air will clear my head," he thinks to himself. The new king steps out to his terrace. The air is frigid and a white layer of snow covers everything. Ollie wraps the blanket tighter around him and races back inside, pulling the door shut.

"Brrrrrr!" He adds yet another log to the fire. Ollie looks from side to side at the room. It is lovely, but oddly, he misses his boot house. It will take time for the palace to feel like home. Ollie makes his bed because that is a good way to start the day. Getting something done makes him feel better.

"I wonder if a king is supposed to make his own bed? I don't want to break the rules," he thinks. But then he chuckles under his breath. "A king is the one who makes the rules. That's cool!" he decides.

Just then Ollie gets a grand idea. "I feel comfortable in my old boot house. I could enjoy a cup of tea there right now!" He puts his hands together and a smile returns to his face. He skips merrily from his bedroom to party sounds coming from the great hall.

The room with the large pillars and shiny floors is filled with mice. Thanksgiving was the first holiday celebrated within the new kingdom, and Ollie made his first decree of no working during that time. The mice had all enjoyed games, music and dancing, feasting and laughter. But that was over yesterday. Today is not a holiday.

A lively group circles around a few mice who are dancing

a jig. "Hey look at me!" one mouse brags as he swings from the chandelier high above.

A tall, half-eaten cake lies within a mess of cups and saucers and napkins. The floor is covered with frosting footprints.

"King Ollie! King Ollie!" The music and dancing stop and the mice crowd around their king.

"Good morning to you all. Is the holiday still going on? Did I miss something?" Ollie asks, looking to the group. As the members of the party look to one another their smiles begin to fade.

Everleigh speaks up. "King Ollie, we didn't know what job to do. We are all so cold, and dancing warms us up."

Sailor pleads and pulls Ollie to follow, "Would you dance with us?"

"Of course I will. I love to dance."

The music begins and the tiny king dances a jig while the mice clap and cheer. He bows at the end of the tune, then pats Sailor's head before continuing to the boot house.

Ollie is beginning to understand. He is not the only one who doesn't know what to do.

On his way to his boot house Ollie finds mice scrambling in every direction carrying armloads of twigs and sticks.

"King Ollie we may freeze! Why is the castle so cold?" Maddox asks before running into another scampering mouse.

"So sorry," a young mouse apologizes before rushing away.

Ollie doesn't know the answer. A group drags a mattress loaded with blankets across the floor. Suddenly Ollie notices many of the blue stars have faded.

Ollie is soon glad to find warmth inside his boot house. A roaring fire is making the tiny home toasty and comfortable. A couple of teacups lie around and a cabinet is left open.

"Rocky must be staying here," Ollie thinks.

Cleever knocks just as the tea kettle is singing. "Come in."

"Burrrrr, the castle is very cold." Cleever rubs his hands together to warm them.

"Good morning friend. Yes, winter is here."

"Your Highness, may I share an observation?"

Ollie's response is interrupted by a visit from Hazel and a mini Karibou.

"Good morning Ollie, we've been looking for you," the pink ladybug announces.

"Yes, I left the castle for the comfort of my old boot house. Please join me for some tea?"

Cleever interrupts. "King Ollie, I need to . . ." but Ollie stops him.

"Cleever, could I visit with you later?"

"Certainly, Your Highness," the mouse sighs and leaves the warmth of the boot house.

Karibou's thick coat is perfect for this climate, and he

sits happily on Ollie's soft chair, but Hazel's whole body is shivering.

"Hot tea will warm you up. What brings you over this fine morning?" Ollie tries his best to sound chipper.

"We both have news," Karibou announces. "I'm not cold, but a spot of tea sounds nice."

Ollie pours the hot drink for them both.

"Let's start with your news Hazel," Ollie tells them while blowing the swirling steam rising from his teacup. Hazel sips her tea.

"Ahhhh, this is delicious. Nobody in the kingdom makes a cup like you, my friend. Thank you. Ok, the big news is this: Twenty-five students are enrolled at Jana Indiana's Drama Academy!" Hazel sits straighter and grins with pride.

"Why Hazel, that is wonderful. I had no idea so many mice were interested in the arts!"

"Neither did I! *The Nutcracker* is to be our first performance." Hazel claps her hands as she says those words with a smile that squeezes her eyes closed.

"Hazel, what exiting news!"

"In all the years I held the summer theatre workshop I never had any students. I can barely contain my excitement. We begin rehearsing right away!"

The pink ladybug then pinches herself. "I just had to do that. It doesn't seem real!"

All three friends share a laugh.

Karibou goes to the window as mice rush every which way.

"What is going on here Ollie? What is happening to your kingdom?"

"What do you mean friend?" Ollie hides his concern by taking another sip of his tea.

"That!" Karibou says, pointing out the window at the madness. Hazel's smile is suddenly soured. Ollie keeps his cup to his lips but his eyes look over the rim at his friends. He sets his tea down and takes a deep breath, and shakes his head.

"What am I going to do? Yes, everything is willy-nilly. I am supposed to be a king, but I am not really certain how to do that." Ollie wrings his hands.

Hazel studies Ollie and looks to Karibou with concern. She has never seen Ollie this way.

Ollie goes to the window. Cleever waits outside with his arms wrapped around himself to stay warm. Ollie motions for him to come in.

"Cleever, let me get you some tea. What were you wanting to tell me?" Ollie asks him while pouring.

"Your Highness, I think the blue stars are fading. The teamwork from last week is gone and the castle is so cold. Could the three things be connected? Everything felt right when we were all working together. Everyone knew what they were supposed to do and the blue stars kept multiplying. And one more thing I've noticed. I think someone is living in your boot house. I asked Rocky and it's not him." Ollie

explores the boot house. The bed has been slept in and his tub shimmers with tiny flecks of red and green.

"I think you are right Cleever. How bright you are to notice these things." Cleever grins from the king's praise.

"You haven't told me your news, Karibou."

"Winter has come to Fort Osage Farm, and according to Fenwick, we are in for a dilly of a snowstorm. I just thought you should know. Farmer Bob and Honey worry that a big snow will keep families from visiting the farm to choose their perfect tree. And one more thing. The two are planning the first Christmas Show to be held at the new Lodge. Honey will serve frosted sugar cookies, children will dress as angels, snowmen or reindeer to perform."

Karibou continues, "They have been practicing for weeks, and now, with this snowy forecast, the show might be cancelled."

"Let's hope not! What fun it will be! We must have a watch party so everyone in the kingdom can enjoy it from the rafters!" Hazel says with excitement.

"I have work to do, King Ollie. Please excuse me." Cleever leaves and Ollie pauses at the window for another look at the mess his kingdom is in.

"I wish my mother were here. This blizzard is dangerous to field mice. Even though I have many problems to deal with, I am most concerned about her."

It is hard for Hazel to see Ollie this way. The little ladybug goes to her friend. She puts her arm on Ollie's shoulder.

"Ollie, it is not like you to be discouraged, but it is easy to see why. I have a bold idea!" She has their full attention.

"Think like a king! You may not feel like one, but I'm asking you to think like one. What would a king do?"

Ollie is quiet for a moment. He looks out the window again. He paces the floor of his boot house.

"A king would be courageous. To fix a problem, one must know all about it," Ollie announces, with strength returning to his voice.

"Exactly!" Hazel says, coaxing him to continue.

"Follow me. In order to make things better, we must know everything!" Ollie takes a clipboard and pencil then leads the group out into the frigid air. Joleen, the king's special jeep driver, waits for him.

The three friends ride in the back. Ollie spots Cleever.

"Cleever hop in and take some notes, would you please?" The mouse drops his arm load of sticks and joins them in the jeep.

"Please write this down," Ollie says to Cleever. "The castle is cold, and the blue stars are fading."

Ollie somehow feels better just saying it out loud.

"Joleen, give us a tour!"

Chapter 3

The driver winds the key until it's tight, then hops back in the jeep. He lifts the lever, jerking the toy car into motion around the village square.

A bright colored beach ball floats in the water of the fountain. Drink cups, towels and leftovers from a picnic lie near the water. Scraps of cardboard from house building scatter the once tidy street.

"Stop!" Ollie tells the driver. "Cleever, please make a list . . . handle trash problem . . . rules for swimming in the fountain."

The small brown mouse scribbles on the paper and the jeep moves again. Two families of mice camp near the green house. They sit huddled around a campfire.

Mia speaks out. "Our house is not built yet."

Markus and Mikael yell out in unison, "We love not working, King Ollie!" Ollie smiles politely and turns to his list maker.

"A place for those without homes yet."

"And maybe some kind of new schedule for workers," the ladybug adds.

The king agrees, "Good idea, Hazel."

Cleever jots on his paper again. Ollie scratches his head.

"They all seemed so happy to be working before."

Victor the gardener approaches the jeep. "Everyone is hungry. They took most of the vegetables, Ollie! It will take some time for me to grow more."

"Don't worry Victor. We will fix this problem. I will have some answers for you."

The jeep continues and Cleever speaks up. "Food supply issues?"

Ollie nods. "Yes."

Just then a mouse comes running from the school.

"Fire! Fire!" Smoke pours from one window. Ollie grabs a bucket from the greenhouse and fills it with water, Hazel and Karibou do the same. They rush in and douse the fireplace flames.

"This fireplace wasn't ready yet . . . a real fire hazard!" Hazel exclaims.

"I know it wasn't finished. I only wanted to stay warm. Look at that wall! It is ruined and school should have started two months ago!" Easton cries.

"We can rebuild a single wall. No tears now. Join your neighbors to keep warm. I will address these problems," Ollie tells the upset mouse.

Cleever knows what Ollie is thinking.

"Fire department, proper fireplace building, school schedule."

"Right again," Ollie nods.

Joleen delivers them back to the castle. Inside the hall the party is over and the group huddles together with their blankets. Some hold their tummies.

"What is wrong?" questions Karibou.

"We are sick," Malorie murmers.

"We ate too much cake," Layton moans.

"Proper nutrition." Cleever suggests, already writing.

"Everything will be alright," Ollie tells them then and leads Hazel, Karibou and Cleever to the royal kitchen.

The room is no longer spic and span as it once was. The fire sizzles and smokes each time soup drips from a bubbling pot. Heaps of dishes and pans wait to be washed. The floor is splattered with spills.

Claire and Grace, the junior chefs, run to Ollie.

"We are so glad to see you!" Grace bursts out.

Claire chimes in, "She's right, King Ollie!" But then she leans in to whisper her next words.

"We are a little worried about Rocky." Claire uses her head to motion towards the royal chef.

A dazed Rocky removes cupcakes from one of the ovens. His once puffy chef's hat is almost limp and hanging on one side. Rocky's apron is smeared with chocolate and caramel and his face is white with flour dust. He sets the tray down and turns to address the king.

"Good morning. Oh excuse me," Rocky says when he notices the sand in the hour glass is empty. He rushes to one of the ovens and removes pastries to cool. He takes off his apron to shake hands with the king, but another dirty apron lies under the first. He laughs nervously.

"Forgive me, Your Highness I am in the middle of . . ." He is cut off again when the sand in another timer runs dry and he stops to check an oven full of tarts. "They need another few minutes."

He turns to the king and removes his apron but yet another apron lies under it. Again, Rocky laughs nervously, Grace rolls her eyes and Claire looks to Ollie with raised brows.

The king stops the madness. "Claire and Grace, tend to timers. Rocky take off all your aprons and sit over here with me."

Rocky removes one apron after another and finally sits with the king.

"I do feel a bit faint. Am I doing a good job, Ollie? I am trying to keep up. I know things are messy but . . ."

The king cuts off his sentence. "Who are you making all of this food for? Our feast is over."

"This is what the royal kitchen does. See here, Ollie," Rocky explains, showing him images from a book on the table. Ollie, Karibou, Hazel and Cleever study the picture from the storybook showing tables piled high with every imaginable food and dessert. Rocky wipes his brow.

"Rocky, I must apologize to you. We forgot to talk about who you will be cooking for," Ollie tells him.

"Well, I just assumed from the hundreds of guests in the great hall at Thanksgiving, I would be feeding the kingdom. I want to do a good job, Ollie. I don't want to let you down."

Before Ollie can ask, Cleever comes to his side with the clipboard and says aloud what the tiny mouse is thinking. "Let the royal kitchen know who they are cooking for and when."

"Yes, that is good, Cleever."

"Perhaps Claire could talk with you about the menu and any upcoming events and make some kind of calendar. She can let Rocky know what needs to be prepared and when. She could have a title of kitchen manager."

"Great suggestion, Cleever!" Rocky looks relieved, Claire looks happy but Grace crosses her arms and smirks.

"Don't worry Grace, there will be plenty of new titles," Ollie reminds her.

"But wait Ollie." Rocky points out. "The picture in the storybook is not the only reason I was making all this food. When I leave the cakes and pastries and tarts on the table at night, they are all gone in the morning!"

Grace speaks up. "You mean this?" she opens a broom closet door. A trash can is filled with leftovers of Rocky's delicious creations.

Karibou examines more closely. "Someone licks all the frosting off and leaves the rest!"

"Well, my recipe is remarkable," Rocky admits, holding his chin. Both Claire and Grace roll their eyes again.

Cleever speaks up, "This is what I mean, King Ollie. I have been finding clues around the kingdom. We are not alone!"

Just then the group hears screams coming from the great room.

"Rocky do NOT make any more food. Please work together to return the royal kitchen to order and wait for my orders on how to go on from here!"

Ollie rushes out and finds a mob gathered in the great hall. Karibou runs ahead.

"Back up, make way for the king," the white dog pleads. When the crowd parts the new king discovers what all the noise is about. Someone is sprawled out on Ollie's throne!

"Zzzzzzzz schewwww, zeeeeeeee shewww," snores a little man wearing a glittery green tunic, red and white striped tights and a leather belt.

"What is that?" Karibou cocks his head to one side.

"What's on his feet?" Rehleigh points to the odd shoes with curled toes.

"He looks like a Christmas elf," Rylon and Parker blurt out. Everyone opens their mouths and raises their brows in wonder.

Ollie taps him gently. "Excuse me, excuse me, please wake up."

The elf's little arm falls limp and a glowing blue crystal stick rolls to the floor, causing everyone to jump back. Ollie

picks it up and examines it. The liquid center is filled with miniature blue stars.

"He is ill!" Hazel notices his pale face. "Let's get him to a bed. He needs help."

Paisley spreads her blanket on the floor. Aspen and Bristol, along with Austin, Hunter and Gabriel, drag the elf.

"Follow me to the guest rooms," Ollie leads the way. Once the stranger is tucked into the bed he moans, then searches his pocket. When he can't find what he's looking for, his eyes grow big.

"Where is it, where is it?" the elf quickly pats at his pockets. Ollie realizes he is talking about the strange blue stick.

"Is this what you are looking for?" The elf breathes a sigh of relief when he sees the object and tucks it back into his tunic.

"I am thirsty," he struggles to say. He pulls a small box from his other pocket and hands it to Ollie. Ollie reads the label, "Christmas Cheer Holiday Spiced Tea." Hazel snatches the box and opens it. Immediately the smells of cinnamon and orange fill the air. For a moment Ollie and his friends are hypnotized by the magical aroma.

Cleever fetches a kettle of hot water and Hazel mixes a cup for the ill stranger. Ollie gently lifts the elf's head, and he sips the heavenly brew.

"That's better."

The elf's eyes flutter just before he falls fast asleep.

"Let him sleep and we will check on him later." Ollie says, then turns to Cleever.

"Find someone to sit with him and give him anything he needs. Then join us in my private quarters with your clipboard. Karibou and Hazel, come with me."

Thinking the weather is now clear, Ollie hopes sunshine will brighten their moods. The mouse king leads them outdoors to his terrace, but the snow is deeper and the wind sweeps Ollie's crown from his head and nearly blows it over the edge. Karibou chases after it.

Just then their attention turns to the turbulent skies and to screams.

Chapter 4

The Hummer Airways plane, filled with passengers, is struggling to fly in the storm. The hummingbird's wings are almost frozen and the plane dips and dives in the sky.

"Stay the course men, stay the course!" Captain Cagney calls out to his team.

The pilots lower their heads and power through the strong winds. They are determined to deliver their passengers safely. One hummingbird tangles with the tallest branches near Ollie's terrace and the plane dips dangerously. Travelers are stopped from spilling out only by their safety belts.

A wing man flying along helps the tangled pilot, and the aircraft continues through the skies, making its final descent to the airport.

Karibou, Hazel and Ollie rush from the palace and ride in the jeep to the village square. The mouse king skips the elevator and races up the three rickety flights of stairs to Hummer Airport. A group of mice gathers at the window hoping for a safe landing. The plane dips to one side, then another. Captain Cagney calls out the order but knows they won't make it safely through the opening.

"Nose up men, nose up! We must circle back around. Stay the course, stay the course!"

Captain Cagney blows a warning whistle so the pretty red hummingbird Rosie can alert everyone.

"Clear way back. We are expecting a bumpy landing. Behind the yellow line! RUN!" The plane battles the weather to reach the open window before vanishing behind a snowy curtain. The watching mice gasp and hug one another. The wind carries the faint sound of Captain Cagney's voice.

"Wingmen, wingmen! Get behind the plane, increase your speed and push!"

Suddenly the wobbly plane emerges from the blinding blizzard headed straight for the airport window. The mice hold their breaths as the aircraft makes it to the runway and comes to a bumpy stop.

The crowd rushes to the freezing passengers. Ollie helps Captain Cagney out of his harness.

"That storm came out of nowhere!" Captain Cagney shakes the snow from his feathers. "We nearly lost it!"

Cessna, one of the other pilots, speaks up. "I wasn't worried, Captain. It was exciting!" Another pilot, Jett, nods in agreement.

Joleen wraps warm quilts around the passengers after they are helped out of their seats. Hazel and Karibou guide the other pilots out of their harnesses and offer blankets. Rosie brings a tray of hot tea to pass out while Cleever closes the panels of the large window. He brings his clipboard near Ollie.

"Airport is closed in poor weather?"

King Ollie nods with concern.

"Exactly, Cleever." After Ollie sees the mice are being cared for and the hummingbirds warming themselves by the fire, he returns to the palace.

Hazel watches as Ollie's shoulders drop. He sighs heavily.

"King Ollie, it has been a rough day. Why not lie down in your chambers for a quick nap? When problems are pressing it can be helpful to step away for a bit. I will bring the clipboard to you in an hour. We can talk about solutions then."

Ollie knows Hazel is right. He heads quietly to his room.

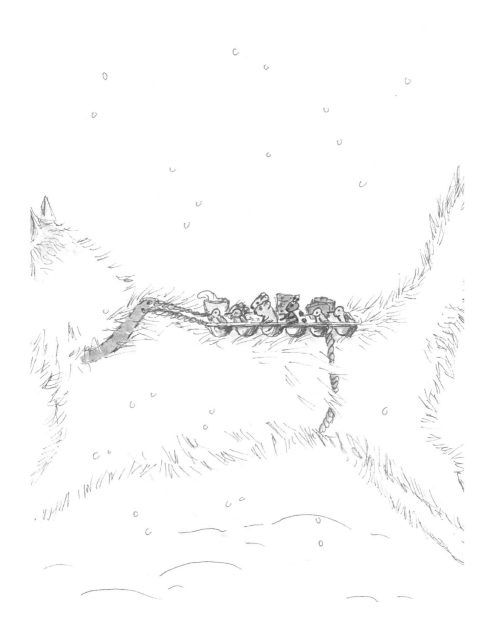

Chapter 5

Hazel needs some time to think, so she and the now tiny Alaskan Malamute puppy go back to the boot house.

"Allow me to mix up one of my famous hazelnut lattes, Karibou! Don't forget, I'm a barista as well as an actress."

"Is that some kind of royalty?" Karibou asks, bringing a giggle from the pink ladybug.

"You are thinking of baroness. A barista mixes fancy coffee drinks. I'm a genius with a coffee bean. You can enjoy it while I soak in Ollie's tub. That is where I get my best ideas!"

The friendly dog likes the brewed drink, and Hazel soaks and thinks. Then she thinks and soaks. Hazel decides the glitter ring left in Ollie's tub must be from the elf.

"It seems elves like a nice bath too," she says aloud to the white dog in the kitchen. A knock on the boot house door brings a glittery Hazel out to join him. Karibou welcomes two pilots from Hummer Airways, Cessna and Jett, inside.

"Come in. Are you warmed up yet from your flight?" Karibou asks.

"Yes. We have a letter from Ollie's mother."

" It was given to us by DPS (Dragonfly Postal Service) to pass on to Ollie. The envelope was lost in the storm."

"Thank you gentlemen," Hazel nods to them both. "Ollie will be glad to hear from his mother." The two pilots exchange glances and finally Jett speaks up.

"The letter had to be read to discover who it might be for. We think you should see it."

Hazel reads aloud.

Dear Ollie,

There have been no updates from you, son. I am worried. The garage home we once lived in is gone, so I moved all my belongings to a hollow log by the brook in the dell. It is quite drafty and damp. My days are spent putting back as much food as I can find for winter. I had an ample stock until Gunter the Gnome tricked me and left me with nothing.

Please send word of your successes soon.

Love, Mother.

Hazel paces around the boot house kitchen knowing they must find a solution.

"She will not survive this blizzard in her horrible conditions. And the gnome will continue to trick her until he takes everything. We must save her!"

The two pilots look to one another and Cessna speaks for them both. "We would like to go on a rescue mission to find Ollie's mother and bring her to the castle."

Hazel is surprised, knowing the airport is closed.

"You will freeze and the last flight almost went down in the blizzard," she reminds them.

"Yes, we know. Captain Cagney would never allow it. That is why we're coming to you. We have warmed up and eaten some healthy foods. So you could say we are fueled up and ready to go. We will wear the winter coats, hats and scarves you made for us. We are familiar with the dell and know where the gnome lives. We think we can find her."

"But the blizzard! It is dangerous to fly," Karibou reminds them.

"If we can stay warm, we can make it. We are strong. We want to do this."

"You are not going without Karibou and I. We must do this for Ollie and his mother."

The hummingbirds nod. Jett explains, "As long as our return flight has only three passengers, just two pilots will be enough. The plane is waiting, our warm clothing is laid out. We are ready!"

"Let's go!" Hazel declares. "I will pick up my winter gear on the way."

Within minutes the pilots open the big windows of the airport and they fly out into the storm. Both Karibou and Hazel are buckled in, but they grip the aircraft. The gusts nearly take their breaths away. Hazel keeps her eyes shut tightly but Karibou enjoys the high adventure. They fly with the wind and make it to the dell in record time.

When they land, Hazel and Karibou jump out.

"Perfect flight boys! Are you staying warm enough?" Hazel asks.

"I'm toasty," Jett chirps and Cessna nods in agreement.

"Okay, everyone position yourselves. It is hard to see in this blowing wind, so follow my plan. I will face south, Karibou will face north, Cessna you face east and Jett west. Walk 100 steps in your direction. Then turn around and come one-hundred steps back with a report. Hopefully one of us will find her."

They begin. Jett quickly finds a log on his path. He moves into the dark and hollow space. A glowing candle burns next to a round wooden door. Jett uses a heavy door knocker.

"Hello? Is anyone home?" he calls out. "Hello?"

Just as he is about to move away, Ollie's mother opens the door. Right away she is shocked to see a warm weather bird at this time of year.

"Come in out of this storm young man! Winter is no place for a hummer!"

"Thank you, but you are not rescuing me, I am rescuing you!"

Ollie's mother does not understand.

"I am pilot Jett of Hummer Airways, part of a royal mission to bring you back to Ollie's Kingdom. Grab only your essentials. I must tell the others I found you." The little mouse watches the hummingbird in his furry blue coat and hat disappear into the blowing snow.

"Who is it dear?" a voice from deeper in the log calls out.

"It's Ollie's soldiers . . . and they are rescuing us!"

"What on earth?" a taller gentleman mouse joins her near the door.

Jett soon returns with the group. Ollie's mother invites them all in. The gentleman mouse shoves the door shut against a fierce wind.

The hollow log home is as cozy as Hazel expected it would be. Two chairs with furry blankets face a stone mantle. Over the flames a pot of soup simmers and a tea kettle warms. Hazel is anxious to find out who the gentleman mouse is.

"Allow me to introduce myself. I am Jana Indiana, but you can call me Hazel. This is Karibou. We are close friends of King Ollie's. I am so pleased to meet you . . . Queen Mother." Hazel curtseys.

"We are here to take you to the castle. The winter is going to be harsh and long. These are our aircraft pilots, Jett and Cessna."

"Ollie is a king! Ollie is a king! How exciting!" Ollie's mother says, putting her hands together. "But my name is not . . . Queen Mother, its Schara."

Not knowing proper royal ways, she lowers her eyes before curtseying back. The hummingbirds snicker before Ollie's mom breaks the awkwardness.

"Where are my manners?" she continues. "This is my husband, the honorable Dr. Carl G. Proctor."

All four rescuers do their best to hide their surprise.

"I was planning to visit Ollie in the spring, but the gnome took all the food we had stored. He is an awful neighbor. Let's all share some tea, shall we?"

Jett speaks up, "There is no time for tea. The winter comes with a mighty roar. We need to deliver you safely to the palace. If we want to complete this mission we must leave now!"

"May I help you gather your bags?" Karibou kindly offers. Schara looks to Dr. Proctor, then back at the group. Hazel understands what they might be thinking and blurts out.

"Of course, Dr. Proctor will be welcome at the castle. Ollie will be happy. And we need a doctor!"

Schara and Carl are pleased with this news.

"Hurry dear, let's get our things."

The two mice scurry around. They make a small pile of needed items outside the door. The rest of the group works together to drag the aircraft closer to the front door. But in the few minutes they are gone, the pile grows. The weight of the extra person, along with the large amount of items, worries the pilots. Just then the doctor and his wife drag out a cabinet. Hazel can see the problem unfolding.

"Schara, that will be too heavy for the plane to fly. We can't take all of these items. Perhaps we can return in the spring for some of the larger things."

"But this cabinet contains important herbs and tonics, my instruments, healing balms and the like. I could never leave this behind." Carl explains.

"And Lord knows, we could use a good doctor and medicine," Hazel adds.

"I know the answer!" Karibou announces. "I'll be right back." Karibou bounds off rapidly, disappearing in the swirls of blizzard snow. The group waits.

Within moments a giant Karibou reappears.

"What . . . what . . . how . . ." is all Schara can say, staring at the towering white animal. The doctor stands in stunned silence.

"There is no time to waste. We will never be able to fly in these conditions and with all this weight!" Karibou lays down in the snow. "Put the airplane on my back and hook the harnesses to my collar. You will need a rope to lace through the back harnesses and around my belly to hold the back of the plane down. Hurry!"

Doctor Proctor brings ropes and helps Cessna and Jett attach the plane securely to Karibou's back.

"It's as tight as we can make it," Jett comments. "Let's get this plane loaded."

While the others are loading the plane, Schara keeps packing. Both she and the doctor hastily put on heavy winter coats and fuzzy mittens.

"All aboard!" Cessna calls out.

Hazel and Dr. Proctor begin to climb up. Suddenly Schara scurries back into the log home and brings out the large pot of simmering soup from the fire. The hummer's eyes grow wide.

"This nutritious soup will only take one seat. It is delicious and you will thank me later when you are enjoying a hot bowl of it. Take this and buckle it in," she commands.

The two pilots nod without even thinking. They grip the handle with their beaks and fly the pot up to one of the seats. Hazel buckles the soup, preparing it for a bumpy ride. When everyone is seated and buckled in, Jett adjusts his goggles and gives the command.

"Karibou, we are ready for take-off." The majestic animal stands and the passengers grip the sides of the egg carton aircraft.

Karibou lowers his head and begins to trot. Before reaching his full stride he does not even feel the weight attached to him.

The wide-eyed passengers tilt and jerk wildly with the movement.

When the white dog leaps over a snowdrift, the passengers are grateful for the safety belts. Some of the thick soup sloshes out of the pot.

Before long they arrive, cold but safe.

Karibou noses the door of the lodge open and bounds up the stairs to the loft and the front door of Ollie's kingdom.

Chapter 6

As soon as the harnesses are removed, Karibou secretly repeats the magic words, "Mini me" and he is tiny once more.

Cessna and Jett find others to help them get the plane back to the airport before Captain Cagney discovers what they have done.

Hazel asks, "Could you and some of your team show the Proctors to their guest quarters? Once they are settled, bring them to our king. We will be waiting."

The two are led through the palace.

"How beautiful Ollie's kingdom is," Schara declares.

"It is a fine castle," Dr. Proctor agrees.

Ollie's mom points out the mysterious blue stars and he nods knowingly. The two must walk around a pile of trash, and away from a few mice who are arguing.

They walk in silence for a moment. The doctor mumbles to his wife. "It looks like the king could use some help."

Cleever overhears his comment. "We just moved into the castle. Everything was beautiful and orderly. But soon the numbers grew and nobody really knows what to do. Our king needs a support team."

"I am doing what I can." Cleever says. "Your rooms are this way."

Ollie's mother does not respond, but she notices talent and skill in Cleever.

"With so many subjects, how does Ollie know who is who?"

"That's a problem too!" Cleever scratches his head.

Karibou and Hazel find the mouse king in the library.

"How was your nap, Ollie?" Hazel smiles, knowing her secret.

"I am refreshed! My plan . . ." he is cut off by an excited ladybug.

"We have a surprise for you Ollie! Come in," she says loudly towards the door.

Ollie's mother enters, beaming with pride. A surprised mouse king pauses before rushing to her.

"Mother, how is it that you are here? Oh Mother, I am so happy."

She holds his face and looks into his eyes. "I have missed you so! You are king of a castle. I always knew you were a leader. I am very proud of you!"

"Thank you, Mother. I can't believe you are here. Let me introduce you."

"Oh darling, we are already fans of Hazel and Karibou, wonderful friends. They, along with a couple of your pilots, rescued us. They are responsible for us being here!"

Hazel fills Ollie in. "While you were napping, the lost letter arrived from your mother. We didn't think she could survive the winter. We had to act."

"I'm so grateful! Thank you," Ollie nods humbly. He turns back to his mother and the man standing next to her. "Husband?"

"Yes dear, this is my kind husband, Dr. Carl G. Proctor." The doctor bows in respect to Ollie.

"How honored I am to meet Schara's son. I was a friend of your father's, Ollie. He was a great mouse. I want to help take good care of your mother."

Ollie is surprised by this news but respectful of his mom.

"Of course, whatever makes my mother happy!" The doctor holds out his hand to shake. Ollie looks to his mother, then instead offers to embrace the gentleman mouse and he accepts. The group laughs and Hazel claps.

"Welcome to my kingdom. I must admit, the role of king is new to me, and I am learning how challenging the job can be. Everything is . . . out of sorts today, and I have many issues to address." A look of concern comes over his face.

"Nothing can be done on an empty stomach!" Ollie's mom announces. "Cleever would you ask the kitchen to bring us the soup I brought from the dell? It is Ollie's favorite, barley stew!"

"Oh, mother!" Schara winks at her son.

"Wait until you taste this rich recipe, with bits of carrot, celery and onion!" Ollie gushes to his friends.

"Don't forget the sage and bay leaf!" Ollie's mother reminds him.

Before the soup is served Hazel goes to fetch her costume trunk from the drama academy. The castle is still cold, and some of the clothing may be of use. When she returns the table is ready and the soup is steaming from the bowls at each place setting.

Ollie and his mother, Dr. Proctor, Karibou and Hazel are seated. Ollie looks around at the room filled with people he cares for deeply, and suddenly the problems don't seem as big as they once did.

They enjoy the delicious soup. Cleever comes back into the room, a sluggish elf behind him.

"Excuse me, Your Highness. The . . . elf . . . is here."

Ollie slides his chair back and goes to him. His mother and Carl do their best to hide their curiosity.

"You must be hungry. Please sit with us. My mother's soup will fix you right up." Ollie tries to introduce the elf to his mother and the doctor.

"May I present . . . this elf . . . whose name is . . . well I don't actually know his name. I am King Ollie, and these are my friends Hazel and Karibou. This is my mother Schara, and her husband, Dr. Carl G. Proctor. And you are?" Ollie fishes for a name.

The elf with dazed eyes does not respond.

"This elf needs fuel. And I'm afraid the barley soup will not do!" Ollie's mom announces to the surprise of everyone

except her Dr. Proctor.

"Cleever could you ask the kitchen to bring some frosting or icing immediately? Thank you." She turns to her husband and he slides back from the table.

"I'll get my doctor's bag." Ollie's mom moves her chair next to the elf.

"Where is your crystal?" The elf responds by patting near his heart. Ollie is puzzled by his mother's knowledge about elves. Dr. Proctor returns and examines the elf's eyes. He removes the green curled toe shoes, exposing blue feet.

"Just as I suspected. He will need the juice of the elderberry and the seeds of the milkweed," Dr. Proctor announces.

Cleever comes back into the room with a bowl of pink icing. Ollie's mom spoon feeds the elf slowly. Cleever, Karibou, Hazel and Ollie are dumbfounded. After eating several spoonfuls he refuses more.

"I will need my oak chest, I brought plenty of milkweed and elderberry potion," Ollie's mom announces.

"Mother, you know about elves?" Ollie says with a puzzled expression.

"Oh my dear, you don't know everything about your mother," she replies with a wink.

When the chest belonging to Schara is brought into the library the doctor wastes no time in giving the elf a spoonful of the deep purple mixture. In only a few minutes the elf is

looking better.

"Thank you," the small man murmurs and trembles.

"This elf is cold, darling. Let's put the downy jacket on him," Dr. Proctor says to Schara.

"Yes, that is exactly what he needs. The castle is very chilly," Ollie's mother responds and pulls a puffy overcoat from her chest of goodies. "Just finished it this past week. With the harsh winter ahead I thought it might come in handy."

She helps the elf with the garment. "He must sleep for a bit. In a few hours he will need more icing and elderberry potion before we can give him the milkweed treatment. Then he will be as good as new," the doctor announces. He leads the elf back to his bed.

Ollie, Karibou and Hazel are astonished by these two newcomers to the castle and barely say a word while Ollie's mother finishes her soup.

"Shall we have a nice cup of tea?" Ollie suggests.

"I would adore that!" she responds.

Mice clear the table and bring steaming cups of sweet tea. Ollie's mom removes a strange item from her stash of supplies. She makes a pile of the odd pods in front of her. She breaks one of them open. Inside are hundreds of seeds attached to white, fluffy, cotton-like tops. They look like tiny parachutes and some escape and float around the room.

"The milkweed is a wonderful plant," Ollie's mom says as she separates the little brown seeds from the fluff-like

parachutes.

"This puffy white material is called floss. I used it to fill the jacket our friendly elf is wearing. It provides excellent warmth. Everyone in the kingdom will need one."

Ollie's mom continues to separate the seeds from the floss. The pile grows.

"Whatever you stuff with the white floss will also float, perfect for water jackets and the like. It makes a nice stuffing for pillows, mattresses and quilts as well."

Hazel shakes her head over Ollie's mom. She is beginning to understand where Ollie gets his wisdom.

Dr. Proctor joins the group and the conversation. He examines one of the milkweed pods and breaks one open.

"Did you tell them about the other uses besides the warmth the white floss gives?" he asks his wife.

"You go ahead, dear."

"Do you see the milky substance inside? It will sting the eyes, so it must be handled with care. But the white milk is useful for skin conditions, and the roots and leaves in a potion will cure a cough and other ailments," he tells them.

"Ollie, I noticed how cold the castle is. The white floss is also good for fire starting."

"How interesting and helpful to us, Carl." Ollie says, impressed. "Our kingdom is new and wobbly. The food is too rich and many are sick because of that."

"I would like to call on those who are ill. And I may

be able to offer some suggestions to your kitchen. Proper nutrition is a must!" the doctor offers.

Ollie puts his hands together.

"That is splendid! Karibou, would you take Dr. Proctor to visit the ill mice, and then to the kitchen to meet Rocky, Claire and Grace?"

"Sure! Follow me, Dr. Proctor," the fluffy white dog says.

Chapter 7

Ollie adds a log to the fire and paces. His mother sits peacefully pulling the white floss from the milkweed seeds.

"You are troubled my son. May I help you?"

"Yes!" Hazel blurts out then covers her mouth. "Sorry!"

"It is quite all right, Hazel. You are as eager to fix things as I am," Ollie nods and smiles at her.

"What are the most pressing things?" Schara wants to know.

Ollie motions to Cleever who clears his throat and reads the first item.

"The castle is cold."

Ollie adds, "We are not sure why. Our subjects are not prepared for it."

Ollie's mother keeps separating the seeds from the white floss. Without skipping a beat she asks an odd question.

"How long have the blue stars been fading?" Everyone in the room freezes.

"Mother! What do you know about the blue stars?"

"Easy now, son. I will tell you when Carl rejoins us. For now let's talk about the result of those stars fading."

Ollie, still stunned by her comment, scratches his head and exchanges glances with the pink ladybug.

Schara continues. "The castle is unusually cold. Is that right?"

"Yes," admits Ollie.

The mother mouse stops her chore and leans back in her chair, arms crossed.

"All the mice in your kingdom will need clothing, and lots of it. I would be happy to teach them how to sew clothing, but a large group of helpers will be needed."

Ollie calls for his royal needle masters.

Hazel pours more tea and within minutes the door is answered and mice enter.

"Mother may introduce my royal needle masters? This is Maddox, Sailor and Everleigh. I taught them how to sew," he announces proudly.

"I am pleased to meet you," she smiles warmly. "My name is Schara. We need your help."

"We can make mattresses and blankets like there is no tomorrow!" Everleigh glows, and the other two raise their chins with pride.

"That is outstanding, Everleigh. Now we must learn to make clothing. Does that sound interesting? Everyone in the kingdom is cold, and we will be counting on you three for

this important mission."

Sailor begins popping up and down as Schara continues. "I want you to choose twenty others and meet me in the grand hall in one hour. I will bring the needles."

"This is so exciting!" Sailor pops her needle master's cap on her head. The other two do the same.

"I like how you wear your needle in a woodsman's cap, just like Ollie once did! Now everyone will see what you're best at!" Schara turns to the ladybug. "Do you have any feathers in your trunk?"

Hazel rummages through the costumes.

"I sure do!" Hazel adds a golden feather to all three caps.

"What will we be making first? How about vests?" Maddox's eyes brighten with excitement.

"We will be sewing everything," she tells them. "But the first things we will make are green woodsmen's caps with golden feathers. Everyone in the needle master's club will be wearing one! You will be held in high esteem as the club that keeps the kingdom warm and looking their best!"

The three needle masters beam with pride and leave with a zip in their step.

"Mother, you are a genius!" Ollie boasts.

"Nonsense!" she remarks. "You are the one who has built a kingdom of believers from lazy field mice. But a good leader needs a team, and I can help you with that!"

"Continue, Cleever," the little king commands. But Ollie's mother holds her hand up to interrupt.

"Hazel do you have a tie in your trunk, and a vest?" Hazel digs a moment then finds a red bow tie and a gray vest.

Schara turns to Cleever, "You are good at making things orderly. I want you to wear this as your uniform."

Cleever lifts his head a bit higher as Hazel helps him with his uniform.

"You look striking, Cleever!" Hazel comments.

"Instead of reading each item on the list, I'll bet you already grouped some things together," Schara flashes him a knowing look.

"How did you know, Queen Mother?" Cleever asks, looking as if she's read his mind.

"I've seen your type. You are just what Ollie needs. What's on your mind?" Cleever shares his well thought-out plan with gusto.

"Well, most of these problems–like throwing trash everywhere, danger of fire, swimming guidelines and proper building of a fireplace–are all best taken care of by a code of operation. Meaning, how our kingdom should operate."

Cleever removes the pencil from his ear and makes a note. Hazel and Ollie marvel at the little mouse.

Ollie places his hand on Cleever's shoulder.

"You are going to head this Code of Operation club."

Cleever smiles widely and explains more of his idea.

"There should be rules to keep our kingdom safe and healthy." Schara winks at Cleever and nods with approval.

"Our kingdom will be like no other," Hazel pipes up. "We should be kind to all, and spend some of our time helping those who are sick, or in need, and spread good cheer. Perhaps a kindness committee?"

"Wonderful, Hazel!" Schara comments.

"I think I understand what happened," Ollie speaks his mind and paces. "All souls need purpose. When we had a goal to build our kingdom using the vision from my dream, everyone had a reason to pitch in. Once we finished, we all felt like ships without sails. We must set new goals, a new target to hit. That's the answer mother!"

Schara nods.

"I couldn't agree with Ollie more," Hazel comments. "The needle masters left on a cloud! And all this talk of goals and targets has me excited too!"

"Mother, I am so grateful for your suggestions. There is still so much to learn," Ollie decides.

"And when we find ourselves in a new situation, we must also be kind to ourselves. Do you follow, Ollie?" she asks.

"What does that mean, exactly?" Cleever asks Schara, who turns to Ollie, hoping he will answer. Ollie is beginning to understand.

"Do any of you remember when Rocky learned to make biscuits the first time? He burned them and was so disappointed. He wanted to give up. I showed him a little

trick to save the burned biscuits and it turned out just fine. I reminded Rocky that everyone must be patient with themselves. With all new things come mistakes. It is part of growing." Ollie smiles at his wise mother.

"Ollie, the same thing applies to every heart, young and old . . . and even kings," she remarks with a wink.

"You are right mother. I must be kind to myself too. Allow room to make mistakes and learn. It will take time each day to become a better king."

"Yes, Ollie," she tells him, closing her eyes and nodding.

Cleever clears his throat and raises his hand.

"No need to raise your hand, Cleever. Go ahead," Ollie tells him.

"May I share my idea for working?"

"Please do, we like your ideas," the king says.

"Once others find what they are good at, we can ask every mouse in the kingdom to work one half day. For this half day they will receive food and water, a house, firewood and be able to attend school if they like. Plus, they will receive twenty points to spend on anything they wish to buy. They will be the workers who will make our kingdom safe and clean."

Cleever shakes his head, really liking his own idea. Hazel and Ollie like it too.

"What about the second half of the day?" Ollie's mother asks him.

"Each mouse could choose to help on the kindness committee, or earn more points by selling things they make, or selling what they can do, like growing food, or painting houses."

"What a good way to fill the village shops with items to sell!" Hazel puts her hands together. "We can start a bakery, a newspaper, and maybe even a book store!"

Ollie adds, "This would leave part of the day for fun, or to enjoy a hobby or even make things to sell."

Cleever keeps the idea going, "Some eager mice may want to work the whole day and earn more points."

Schara agrees. "And those who work only half a day will still have a house, food and warmth. What a smart plan, Cleever!"

"Who will keep track of the points?" Cleever's eyes look to the ceiling, his mind searching for an answer. Ollie scratches his head then spies the pile of seeds in front of his mother. He grabs a handful of seeds, then lets them drop out, one by one.

"How about using these like coins instead of tracking points? We could use milkweed seeds! All workers who work one half day will get twenty seeds. Merchants in the stores can put a price tag on something they make, and take seeds as payment." Ollie declares.

"Great idea, son! And don't forget about bartering. That could be useful in the kingdom too," Ollie's mother points out.

Cleever is confused by the word bartering.

"What is bartering?"

Schara gives an example. "Let's say a painter needs extra bread for his growing family but he doesn't have enough milkweed seeds to pay for all those loaves of bread. And let's pretend the baker is too busy to paint his own house. The painter could offer to paint the baker's house. Instead of paying the painter with seeds, the baker could offer to bake the extra loaves the painter needs for his family. See how bartering can work?"

"What a great idea! King Ollie, if I may be excused? I want to get some of these things figured out. I can put the ideas together and will bring you my results," Cleever suggests.

"That is wonderful. Thank you, Cleever."

Chapter 8

Ollie and Karibou, Schara and the doctor find the elf sitting up. His eyes are no longer dazed and his cheeks are pink.

"You look much better," Dr. Proctor announces.

"I feel better too!" The little guy flashes a radiant smile, causing the mice to peek through squinted eyes.

"Nice smile!" Karibou mentions.

"Thank you. My name is Jolly McJingles. I come from the North Pole."

"Welcome, I am King Ollie."

"I know who you are, kind Ollie. It was your goodness that led me to help you."

"Are you responsible for the blue stars in my kingdom?" The mouse king is anxious for his answer.

"Yes. I saw the power of your dream in action. How could I not help you?" Jolly smiles humbly.

"When things needed done, I waited until everyone was asleep and finished the jobs. I thought I was helping spread goodness in the world." The elf drops his head.

"You did help us. What you did was wonderful. We are grateful Jolly." Ollie explains.

His words bring a big smile to Jolly's face, and everyone in the room squints. But a sadness returns.

"I am the E.E. and I've let my team down," he murmurs. They don't understand what Jolly means.

"What is the E.E.?" the Malamute dog asks.

"Early Elf. It is an important job. Every elf wants to be the E.E! I am sent from the North Pole weeks before Christmas Eve to holiday places like tree farms to spread magic around."

The elf continues. "Something happens to your heart when you shop for or decorate a tree with loved ones. We provide the magic to keep this spirit alive. I sprinkled blue stars across the gate leading into the farm, so visitors feel the warmth only the magic of Christmas can bring. Each pine tree in the field is graced with a sprinkling of this same magic."

"The blue star over each tree?" Ollie asks.

"Yes, Ollie. Throughout the season as the family gathers around their tree and admires it a holiday joy fills their hearts. I put extra doses of magic over the lodge but soon the other elves on my team will arrive to work the inside of the lodge. Only Christmas elves can add that sparkle of holiday luster. When we spread our magic, the world is brighter, happier and more joy-filled. Ohhhhhhhh, I love what I do!" the elf squeals.

Ollie's mom speaks up.

"But now you are having a problem with your crystal, aren't you, Jolly?" Schara touches his arm tenderly. The glittery elf nods slowly. He reaches in his vest and pulls out a softly glowing stick. Karibou and Ollie are puzzled.

"May I?" Schara carefully takes the crystal object. "This crystal is sent with elves to spread Christmas magic. When I entered your castle Ollie, I recognized the blue stars as elf magic. We have seen it before."

Both she and Dr. Proctor nod. Karibou and Ollie hang on every word as she goes on.

"Jolly used almost all his Christmas magic to help create your kingdom, and there is not enough left. That is why the stars are fading."

"Yes," Jolly admits.

"You helped us. Now allow us to help you," King Ollie says.

"But you don't have the Christmas magic," Jolly McJingle shakes his head then continues.

"I'm not sure you understand. We make Christmas trees more beautiful, the decorated mantle more dazzling, holiday treats more delicious, the family love stronger, but not on this farm this year."

Ollie listens and thinks for a moment before responding. "I have a kingdom of mice who are good and kind. We will become part of your elf team. We will shine every bulb, polish every ornament, clean every pearl, dust every tree skirt, and make this lodge shimmer with our own brand of magic."

Ollie stops to catch his breath before going on.

"If that is all we can do, then let us do it the best we can. When families come inside, they will feel the love we showered over every detail. It may not be the same magic, but we will not stop until this place is a beautiful as we can make it. Please let us help, Jolly!"

"The rest of the elves will be here tomorrow night. I guess you all will be part of our team," he tells them. Ollie's support brings a big grin to Jolly's face, causing the mice to squint a little. His smile reminds the doctor of something.

"The mice in this kingdom are eating too much sugar. Most of the patients I've examined have dull teeth, not bright white teeth like our friend Jolly. I will be teaching the good habit of brushing our teeth so we can all have smiles like Jolly," the doctor says.

"Oh yes, we brush with our special toothpaste," Jolly says.

"Tell me about it!" the doctor exclaims.

"We use chocolate toothpaste. It is delicious, and makes brushing something we want to do often. I would be happy to share tubes with all the mice," the elf offers.

He flashes his bright smile, causing everyone to squint again.

"Don't worry, you'll get used to it!" he says, and they all chuckle.

Chapter 9

After a few days pass, Jolly, Karibou, and Ollie leave the palace in the loft attic and find a safe place to watch the action going on in the grand hall.

"Look!" Karibou exclaims.

Far below, Honey and Farmer Bob are surrounded by boxes of garland, Christmas trees, ornaments and gift items. Honey has been decorating for hours. The mantle over the fireplace is decorated with boughs of pines, gold and red bulbs and a strand of lights.

"What's going on?" Ollie asks the elf.

"The new grand hall is going to be used as a gift shop this season. They are calling it The Lodge."

The three look over the mess while Honey crosses her arms and stares at the mantle.

"Something is missing," she decides. "The white twinkle lights seem dull."

"Maybe the light strand needs replacing," Farmer Bob suggests.

"I just bought all new ones. I can't put my finger on it, but this new lodge is lacking something." Honey's shoulders drop.

"The Lodge will be wonderful," Farmer Bob puts his arm around her. "Especially since we are hosting our first-ever Fort Osage Christmas Show! Our visiting families will enjoy the show. Imagine the glow of the fireplace as young performers sing and dance and act on our little stage. The place will be filled with angels, snowmen, hot cocoa, spiced tea and plenty of Christmas spirit."

"It does sound like fun," Honey agrees. "I love our plan of painting a holiday mural on the wall behind the stage. That will set the mood. When will the artist be coming?"

"In the next few days, if this snow lets up," Farmer Bob glances out at more falling snow.

"You know how important good weather is. If there is too much snow, families won't be able to make it here and we won't have the Christmas show!" Honey plops down on the fireplace hearth.

Farmer Bob sighs. "We can't control the weather, and worry won't change a thing. Let's get the rest of these decorations up and quit for the day." Farmer Bob's words put a smile back on Honey's face.

"Honey and Farmer Bob will need all the help they can get," Ollie tells Karibou and Jolly.

"And even with everyone helping, this lodge will be missing our Christmas magic," Jolly mentions.

"That will hurt Fort Osage Farm," Karibou says with sadness.

"We will do all we can. Time for us to welcome the other elves," the mice king tells them.

Chapter 10

Hazel meets up with the king, Jolly and Karibou on their way to the palace's grand hall. Curious mice circle around the sparkly elf. Jolly passes out tiny red and white striped candy canes.

The ladybug questions Ollie while they wait.

"Will your mother and the doctor be joining us for dinner?"

"Not tonight. They are helping Cleever with the new water tower."

"The kingdom is really shaping up. In only a few days everyone is working again. They are happy with the new system Cleever and his team introduced."

She adds, "When I was in the village square, I noticed the bakery had a few pastries in the window for sale."

"That is good news, Hazel. We are making progress." Ollie points his finger in the air.

"Did someone mention news? Is there news?" a mouse wearing a fedora and carrying a small notebook asks.

"Allow me to introduce myself. I'm Gidget—editor, reporter and photographer of Gidget's Gazette. I'll be covering the happenings here in Ollie's kingdom."

"Do you have time for a few questions?" she asks.

Before Ollie can respond, Gidget blurts out another question. "Is this the elf? Is it true a whole team of elves is expected?"

Ollie is caught off guard. "Yes," he answers slowly.

"Will your kingdom become the new North Pole? Will Santa arrive soon?" Gidget shoots questions off so fast Ollie is confused.

Hazel takes over.

"Gidget dear, Ollie would love to be interviewed tomorrow over tea. Let's say 2 p.m.? See you then."

"But my deadline! How about a quick photo?" Gidget looks at the group through a black box while holding something over her head. "This is my own pinhole camera and flash lamp . . . made it myself. Smile!"

POOF! FLASH! A small blast of smoke comes from her lamp. The mice blink, blinded by it for a moment, which gives Gidget a chance to dash away. "Thank you, Your Highness. See you tomorrow!"

"I guess there is now a newspaper!" Ollie says with a grin.

Junior chefs Claire and Grace greet the four when they reach the great hall.

"Good evening, King Ollie. This way please," Grace points towards the table. The cluster of candles rising from the middle of the table gives off a pleasant glow, and place

settings shimmer in the flame's light.

"Be seated and enjoy elderberry juice until the elves arrive," Claire announces.

"Good work, Claire and Grace," Ollie praises.

Hazel notices their soft blue uniform tops and chef hats. "Very nice. You two look the part." The two junior chefs stand proudly, waiting to serve.

Suddenly the ground vibrates. The chandeliers overhead begin to clink and jingle, and their candle flames grow tall, nearly reaching the ceiling.

"It's happening! They're here!" Jolly dives under the dining room table.

"Jolly, why---?" Before Ollie can finish his question a brilliant ball of sparkles swirls, pops and crackles. Karibou ducks under the table just as it explodes.

Elves shoot out from the ball and fall through the air before tumbling to a stop in every direction. A smoky haze remains. The elves cough and sputter as they come to their feet.

"Jolly, what's up with this rumbly ride? JOLLY?" The little guy crawls out from under the table to answer.

"I'm sorry Cider, I ran into a few problems," he reports, his eyes lowered.

Suddenly other elves rush to Jolly and all talk at once. "We missed you Jolly!" When the elves smile, their teeth are so bright the mice must squint again.

"The North Pole is not the same without you," one remarks. Each of them wears a sparkly tunic of various colors, red and white striped tights, and green shoes that curl over their toes.

The mouse king comes to the group.

"I am King Ollie. Welcome to my kingdom," he spreads his arms wide. Jolly starts the introductions.

"This is Goldie Von Glitter," Jolly touches the shoulder of her gold tunic.

"Greetings to all!" Goldie bows.

"This is Sugar O'Sprinkles," the elf bows. His silver tunic shimmers.

"In the powder blue tunic is Frosty FitzCinnamon, and in the dazzling bronze is Cocoa DeCaramel. Finally, in snow white, is Cider Saint Snowflake."

Each bows respectfully. Tiny bells jingle from the tips of their curled toe shoes and the points of their hats.

"Let's get started, shall we?" Cider announces.

"Wait, we would like to share our dinner with you. Please sit with us."

"That is so very kind of you, King Ollie," says Cocoa.

After everyone is seated, royal chef Rocky waits as Claire and Grace roll carts near the table.

"For our new friends, we have our own special tea blend, 'Christmas Cheer.' It is a cinnamon sweet tea, sure to become a favorite. We also will be serving a new recipe . . . cotton

candy bonbons." Rocky points to the colorful item.

"Light pink and blue puffs of cotton candy on a stick, with a surprise creamy center of white chocolate." The elves raise their brows in fascination.

"Wait, there's more!" Rocky exclaims. "I am serving chocolate lasagna! Rich layers of milk chocolate, a few layers of marshmallow cream, all covered with a delicate French vanilla bean icing, dusted with crushed candy canes!"

The elves begin to clap, eager to taste these royal delicacies.

"We are impressed already!" bubbles the silvery-clad Sugar. "We just left the island of misfit toys and were given sugar packets with straws. Quite delicious, but not as fancy."

Rocky blushes as Claire and Grace help serve the guests.

"For the rest of you, there is sweet potato and walnut pie, sunflower soufflé and elderberry tarts with cream."

"I am hoping to sample one of those cotton candy bonbons!" Hazel announces.

Karibou agrees, adding. "Chocolate lasagna, that sounds yummy! Too bad dogs aren't supposed to eat chocolate."

"You have outdone yourself Rocky, Claire and Grace! Bravo!" Ollie cheers.

While everyone enjoys the meal Goldie brings up the subject Jolly was avoiding.

"How is the crystal? Are we in good shape to finish our mission at Fort Osage Farm?"

The elves keep enjoying the sugary food, but everyone else is silent as they hear Jolly explain.

"Well, that is the 'hiccup' I was talking about. I've made a very--"

Ollie feels responsible for the E.E.'s situation and speaks up. "I'm afraid there is news to share. You see, from a young age I dreamt of being king of a castle. None of us has ever lived anywhere but humble homes in boots and under logs. From my vision, this kingdom was built. Jolly saw everything and used most of the magic in the crystal to help us make this palace and kingdom. I am so sorry." Ollie apologizes.

"But how will we create Christmas magic at Fort Osage Farm?" Frosty wonders before being interrupted by Cocoa.

"HOLD EVERYTHING! This tea is like nectar. It is the best tea ever! I love Christmas Cheer!" The other elves agree, drinking to the bottom of their cups and asking for more. The mouse king nods and sips it too. He turns back to answer Frosty's question.

"We will help you," Ollie promises. "We are not magical like you, but we believe in the power of dreams. We will begin tomorrow. My entire kingdom of mice will dust, polish and shine, giving the Lodge a special Christmas sparkle."

The elves look to one another with concern. Ollie continues, "We cannot change the amount of magic in the crystal, but we can give one hundred percent of our hearts. Will you let us try?" Ollie pleads.

"Of course Ollie! We will work together." Cider looks to

the other elves who nod, their mouths full of cotton candy bonbons and chocolate lasagna.

Cider answers for them all, "Okay, as long as Rocky will feed us more of his delicious creations, we accept your offer of help!"

Just then each elf loads a small brush with chocolate toothpaste. They politely turn their backs and brush their teeth in only seconds.

Ollie makes his announcement while squinting from their bright smiles.

"Wonderful! Tomorrow we will begin!"

Chapter 11

The next day is an exciting one in the Lodge at Fort Osage Farm. Goldie, Sugar, Frosty, Cocoa, Cider and Jolly form teams to make everything as magical as they can.

Goldie leads the Sparkle Team. Hazel suggests all squad members wear royal blue dazzle overalls. Rehleigh, Rylon, Parker, Paisley, Aspen and Bristol follow Goldie's lead.

They begin with the mantle over the fireplace. She shows them how to remove each tiny bulb in the string of lights. Goldie uses a special fabric to clean the bulb and create a luster. The crew uses mini feather dusters to clean evergreen boughs. They next sprinkle them with a glistening snow dust.

A few of the mice tote buckets filled with warm water and a cleaner that smells like fresh-from-the-oven chocolate chip cookies. They use it to shine the ornaments to a brilliance.

Sugar O'Sprinkles leads a group of volunteers into the kitchen pantry of the Lodge. She explains to her crew, "We add more. Our mission is called Add-To-It."

Austin scratches his head. In unison Hunter and Gabriel ask, "What is that?"

"Add-to-it. We are looking for ingredients used in common Christmas recipes. We make cinnamon more spicy, brown sugar sweeter, butter more creamy, chocolate chips a

bit bigger. We put a boost of vanilla in the bean, we add extra stripes to the canes! Do you get the idea?"

Some of the mice nod and she continues. "We plump the sugar plums, glaze over the cookies and we super shine every confection!"

"Wow! That sounds awesome!" Justin nudges his brother Kole. Sugar winks at the two mice. "You twins look so much alike, I may not remember your names."

"We are not twins," Kole scuffs the floor.

"From now on I will group some of you together. Will you help me make things easier?" she asks. She points at the two mice boys. "If I call out 'twins,' I'm talking to you two, okay?" They both nod.

Three boys, Weston, Waylon, and Wyatt, have toppled a salt shaker and ride it like a horse. "You three will be called the wranglers. Let's go!"

Meanwhile, Frosty FitzCinnamon gathers his group. Markus, Mikael, Hudson and Mia join with Layton, Easton, Malorie, Domonic and Zoey.

"We need a name!" Markus calls out.

"And hats!" Mia adds.

"Hold on everyone. Our smiles will be our uniform!" Frosty grins widely and the white glow of his teeth cause some of the mice to step back.

"I have something special for each of you–chocolate toothpaste and brushes from the North Pole!" The team jumps up and down. Frosty teaches them all how to do a

quick brush.

"Okay, now let's see those smiles!" Every mouse in the group shows off his or her best smile. Their white teeth radiate. "Looks like we are ready to do our job!"

"What do we do?" they ask in unison.

"We are the keepers of the flame!" The elf snaps his fingers and a flame burns from his pointed finger. The volunteers gasp, their eyes filled with wonder.

"Every light bulb, candle flame, fire pit, tea light, solar stake, fireplace or lantern will need a hypnotizing glow. The power of the flame can slow people down. The warmth from light finds its way into hearts, young and old. Follow me team!"

Cider Saint Snowfall gathers her group at the rafters above the front door. She hands out small green leaves.

"They are a bit sticky on the back. These are leaves from mistletoe, a symbol of Christmas. You can attach the leaf to your chest, so all will know what team you're on!

"Can we eat them?" Amelia wonders, looking at the leaf. Her siblings and cousins laugh.

"No, we wear them with pride. Gavin, Ashton, Devin, Noah, Lexi and Dylan put your leaves on." As they attach their leaves Cider explains.

"We must shower each twig of mistletoe with devotion. This simple plant brings hearts together in friendship and love. It is a symbol of peace. And then we have another job to do."

Cider holds out a dozen tiny brooms and points to the front double doors. "See the space on the floor? That is called a threshold. All entrances have them. We must sweep all thresholds with care, then we must perform the 'cross-over' jingle on each. Then they are ready for the holidays."

The mice follow the elf to the threshold with excitement. "When families cross over this threshold, we want a feeling of happiness and peace to sweep over them. Come on everyone, sweep, sweep, sweep!"

Cider and the whole team sweep with gusto.

"Is it time for the cross-over jingle?" Devin hopes.

"Yes!" Cider replies. She clears her throat crosses her arms. Then she sings her song while dancing a jig.

Cross over, Cross over and lend me your ear.

Christmas is coming, the best of each year.

Leave behind your troubles and woe.

This is the time to let your heart glow.

The group of mice picks up the tune quickly and joins in her singing and dancing.

Cross over, Cross over and lend me your ear.

Christmas is coming, the best of each year.

Leave behind your troubles and woe.

This is the time to let your heart glow.

"Great job, everyone!" Cider praises with a cheery

thumbs-up. "We have lots to do. Follow me!"

Jolly wonders if all these efforts will be enough. With the crystal lacking in magic, he doesn't think so. Ollie, Hazel and Jolly notice the last elf and her group of mice just sitting by the cocoa station below.

"What's going on with Cocoa?" Ollie asks the elf.

"Oh, Cocoa? She waits for inspiration. She doesn't move too fast."

"Inspiration?"

"She enjoys being different. Just watch."

Amelia speaks up. "Are we going to do anything?"

The other mice wait for words from their elf, who is sprawled out on a bed of paper napkins. She yawns.

"I'm waiting," she answers.

"Waiting for what?" Kaycee asks, filing her nails.

"For that big silver thing to heat all the water inside. I usually don't get busy until I've had my cocoa, tea or cider. As soon as that red light comes on . . . wait for it, wait for it . . . there it is!" Cocoa puts several large scoops of Christmas Cheer Tea in a cup and adds hot water from the urn. The steam rises and she inhales the sweet aroma.

"Ahhhhh, now that is what I'm talkin' about!" Cocoa stirs with a spoon almost as tall as she. "See the surprise at the bottom of the cup?" All the mice crowd around the rim and look inside.

"What is it?" they ask her.

"I don't know, but when they melt, the flavor explodes! Pour yourselves some of this Christmas Cheer. It rocks!"

The mice mix one large cup and each uses a straw to sip.

"It's delicious!" Hudson exclaims.

After a few minutes Cocoa stands and starts snapping her fingers to a beat. She closes her eyes, head bobbing in rhythm. Soon a few of the mice do the same, then they all do.

Cocoa is moved by the groove and with her eyes closed she starts to perform. Snap, Snap, Snap . . .

"Cocoa was first just a tiny ol' bean, but she grew to be a player on the holiday scene.

Some would say she's different, some would say she's fine.

But I'm Cocoa the Elf and I'm fun all the time . . . hey, hey

Snap, snap, snap....hey hey, snap, snap, snap . . ."

The group members snap their fingers along with the beat and follow everything Cocoa does. Soon they are all moving with her.

Snap, Snap, snap . . .

"Cocoa was first just a tiny ol' bean but she grew to be a player on the holiday scene.

Some would say she's different, some would say she's fine.

But I'm Cocoa the Elf and I'm fun all the time . . .

Hey hey, snap, snap, snap....hey hey. Snap, snap, snap.

Cocoa continues to snap her fingers with the rest and really gets revved up, but when Jolly catches her eye she quits snapping her fingers, frowns and drops her shoulder.

"Ok, we have to get crackin'."

"But we were having fun!" one of the mice cries.

"I know! But everyone will be done before us and that's not cool. Let's roll!" she shouts.

"What's our job?" they ask in unison. In her dramatic fashion Cocoa explains, using big motions with her hands.

"Well, we make the Christmas Cheer tea irresistible, we make the cocoa richer, we sweeten the cider, we add salt to the salted caramel."

Inspiration comes over her again and she begins snapping her fingers but catches Jolly's eye again and stops her groove.

Suddenly the big double doors open and in with a rush of winter wind comes a woman with bags. She wears a black wool coat and beret. The mice scramble like crazy to hide, but the elves are invisible to most. Ollie and Hazel stand in the shadows of the trusses.

"That must be the artist. She is painting a mural on the wall behind that stage for the Christmas show," Ollie explains.

Chapter 12

The artist cleans the wall and prepares her tools. She stands back to study her blank canvas. With crossed arms she tilts her head from side to side. Ollie spots a mouse he's never seen climbing from one of the bags. She wears a trench coat and even a beret, just like the artist. The mouse king gawks at this newcomer who scampers into the shadows carrying a tiny suitcase. In a couple seconds he sees her again leaping to a crosswalk and making her way closer to them.

"Bonjour!" says the breathless mouse with kind eyes. Hazel looks to the king who only stares at the lovely stranger. "You don't speak French, oui?"

Ollie still does not move.

The ladybug smiles politely as the pretty mouse continues. "No matter, I know your native English. My name is Simone Claudette, artiste, and you?" Simone puts her hand out to shake, her eyes surrounded by wispy lashes.

Hazel shakes her hand. Ollie's eyes widen but no words come from his mouth.

"I am Hazel. Welcome to Fort Osage Farm. This is King Ollie." He blushes and smiles but it takes a nudge from his friend before he responds.

"Hello Simone." The king takes her hand, keeping his gaze on her white teeth and delightful smile.

The silence that follows is awkward and Hazel jumps in again. "You are not from here. What brings you to the Kingdom of Ollie?"

"I come with Lee Jacque," Simone points to the woman painting the mural.

"She is artiste from Paris, and I learn much from her." Ollie is still hypnotized.

Hazel asks, "Is Paris nearby?"

"Pas, no, no. Paris, France, the city of love." She responds. "I see the world with Lee Jacque," she tells them, pointing to her suitcase covered with travel stickers.

Finally the mouse king finds his voice.

"And will you be staying for a time?" He manages to ask in a hopeful tone. The mouse with the beret looks to the artist below.

"I never know how long. When her work is done, we are off again. She will paint well into the night and most of tomorrow, I'm sure."

"Can I offer you a hot coffee or tea? Traveling in this weather must be hard." Ollie uses his hand to direct her toward the attic loft.

"I would love a cup of espresso."

Hazel nearly jumps out of her skin.

"I am a barista, I make a wonderful espresso!"

"I knew I liked you!" Simone gushes. Both females laugh as they walk ahead of a mouse king who trips over his feet in order to follow.

"My drama academy will be doing its dress rehearsal of **The Nutcracker** tonight. Would you like to come?"

"Ahhhh, I adore the ballet!"

"Perfect! I'll make you that espresso," the ladybug tells her.

Ollie shows Simone to one of the guest rooms in his castle. At her door he rushes his words.

"Would you like to dine with toothpaste?" The pretty mouse wrinkles her nose at his odd question.

Ollie's blunder flushes his face. "I'm sorry Simone. Would you like to join me for dinner?" he asks, relieved to even put a sentence together.

"How kind of you to offer. But my work must be done first."

The little king tries hard to hide his disappointment.

"But I will be going to the ballet later tonight, perhaps we can meet there."

"Oh, yes. I will see you then." Ollie smiles at the lovely stranger and once more forgets to talk.

"Adieu," she speaks softly and closes the door and he snaps out of his trance.

"Goodbye." Ollie turns and runs into Cleever.

"Pardon me, King."

"No it was I. I am distracted."

"We are making progress Ollie. The elves and their teams finished most of the work in the lodge. Karibou had a fun idea. Why not all gather on Christmas Eve to enjoy the Christmas Show? High in the rafters of the Lodge is a nice spot for a watch party. The sparkle squad is getting everything ready." Cleever takes the pencil from his ear and makes a note about it. "Have you noticed, sir?"

"What's that, Cleever?"

"The blue stars, they seem to be glowing more brightly again. Perhaps the elf team is the reason."

"Could be," King Ollie mumbles.

Hazel interrupts them both.

"Well, there is a glitch with the dress rehearsal tonight! The stage was getting painted and it will not be dry in time. We must find a stage for our practice performance."

"I have an idea," Cleever offers. You know the landing near the rafters on the attic level? On Christmas Eve we are planning a big watch party. The sparkle squad is decorating it with a tree and garland. Have your dress rehearsal there tonight."

"Great suggestion," Hazel says as Ollie walks back to his room before the ballet.

He spends extra time smoothing the stray hairs between his ears but they pop right back up. Ollie tries something new- a little lavender oil to smooth things down. That does

the trick. He likes the smell and the oil makes his coat sleek and shiny, so he applies it all over.

He practices his smile in the mirror. Dr. Proctor is right, he thinks. Mice do have dull teeth! He takes a brush and piles it high with chocolate toothpaste. Ollie finds it delicious. He can hardly wait to brush again! He rinses his mouth and smiles at his reflection. His teeth are stunning!

Ollie skips around his room. He looks at himself again in a long mirror. He pulls his shoulders back and places his crown on his head. But something is different. Lots of oily hair is sticking up straight through his crown.

Ollie's mom knocks on his door.

"Come in Mother. I am getting ready to attend the dress rehearsal of Hazel's first show. How are you?" He says with a wide, radiant smile.

Schara is stunned by the way her son looks. His hair spikes up like freshly mowed grass. The rest of his coat is matted down and shiny. She chooses her words carefully.

"Your teeth are super white. They look wonderful."

Ollie locks his smile in stiffly. "And your hair, it . . . glistens," she comments. Ollie beams.

He finally lets out a breath and relaxes. His wise mother asks a few questions.

"What did you do today?"

"The elves and their teams worked hard. I hope the Lodge will carry the same kind of Christmas magic the families have come to know from this farm."

"Anything else?"

"The artist came to paint the mural behind the stage for the Christmas Show."

"How exciting. I will look forward to seeing that. Anything more?"

"Not really. I did meet a stranger who came along with the artist. She too is an artist from Paris. Her name is Simone." Ollie's mom observes how he gazes off in the distance after saying her name.

Schara understands, and can see her son needs some help. "I have a gift for you. Why don't you wear this tonight? I was going to wrap it for Christmas, but it's perfect for the ballet." Schara takes a pair of grey flannel trousers and a soft blue sweater from her bag. "Made it myself. I hope you like it."

"Mother, how thoughtful. I will indeed wear them." Ollie begins putting them on but his mother stops him.

"I need to finish a few stiches on the trousers. Why don't you . . . take a soapy bath, and by then I will be done."

"Good idea, Mother."

Chapter 13

The landing has been transformed by the sparkle squad. A stage glistens from dozens of flickering candles. An audience waits for the curtain to rise. Hazel flits about with her clipboard. She flies down to Ollie.

"Oh Ollie, I've never been so excited. The house is packed!"

Hazel notices Ollie's bright smile and his fine clothes. "Oh Ollie, how handsome you are!" Her words make him happy.

Just then Hazel is tapped by Maddox and Sailor, who both carry scripts. Maddox speaks for them both.

"As your directors we need to tell you about a problem backstage. We all know pixies must never chew gum!" Maddox clenches his teeth and raises his brows. Sailor can't stop giggling.

"What's going on?" Hazel asks.

"A pixie from Edgewater Empire showed up demanding the lead role of sugar plum fairy!" Maddox tells her, and Sailor giggles more.

"But Everleigh is the lead and opening night is in a couple days. That is absurd!" Hazel exclaims.

By now Sailor is laughing so hard she can barely speak.

"Everleigh smiled sweetly, but she didn't say anything. She simply offered a piece of gum to the pixie and now her mouth is stuck together!" Sailor holds her belly and laughs. "That pixie looks so funny trying to be mad!"

"And she's really angry!" Maddox blurts out, finally giving in to his giggles.

"That could be bad. One shouldn't anger the pixies," the ladybug says before snickering herself. That just gives the two permission to let their laughs roll.

"Just give them all gum!" Sailor jokes and both she and Maddox fall down in hysterical laughter.

Hazel takes a deep breath and turns to Ollie. "Enjoy the show," she says as she hustles backstage.

"King Ollie, follow me to your special seat." Easton guides him wearing pretty fairy wings. Ollie looks for Simone. His heart sinks a little when he doesn't find her.

The lights go down and the music begins. After some time he glances around again and spots the pretty mouse waving a white handkerchief from up higher. She motions for him to join her. Ollie scampers up the beams to where she is.

"King Ollie, I'm sorry but I couldn't find a seat. This is a perfect place to watch. We can see everything."

"Yes," is all Ollie can manage to say. The sight of the dancers in the soft glow of the candles is magical. Simone follows their every move, and Ollie watches Simone. One

time she catches him looking at her instead of the stage, and she smiles so beautifully that Ollie feels dizzy.

"Can I offer you some Christmas Cheer?" Ollie asks her at the break.

"No, Ollie. Let me show you." She spreads a checkered cloth on the floor. "Sit here King Ollie," she says, patting a spot for him next to her. "I brought grape juice, French bread and some cheese. Perfect for a picnic."

She rips a piece of bread from the loaf and shares it with Ollie. It is delicious.

"How did you become a great king, Ollie?" Simone sips her drink.

"I always dreamed of being king of a castle. I kept working and building and telling others about my dream. I am still learning how to be a good king."

"That is interesting. I've never met anyone like you. Everyone in your kingdom is special."

"Thank you, Simone. Tell me about your home." Ollie enjoys the fine cheese. He sips the sweet juice and when he hiccups, Simone giggles.

"I make my home in Paris above Café de la Paix, a studio where I live and work. When Lee Jacque works all over the world I tag along."

"How is it done? It sounds like an adventure."

"Lee Jacque is a creature of habit. She always travels with the same tools and bags. I found a comfortable spot in

the lining of one bag where I am safe and warm. I smuggle myself to the next exciting place. There is such a big world to see."

Simone takes a small easel from her suitcase. The mouse king is quiet as she paints a scene from the stage. Everleigh is dazzling the crowd with her graceful pirouette.

"Your painting is lovely," he tells her.

The curtain closes but the music keeps playing as the audience makes its way home.

"The enchanting blue stars are like nothing I've ever seen before." Simone says.

Ollie breathes deeply before asking. "Would you like to dance, Simone?"

She smiles at King Ollie and takes his hand. Within the glow of the candlelight they twirl to the Waltz of the Flowers.

Chapter 14

Karibou rests beside Farmer Bob and Honey as they sip coffee in the warmth of their home. Outside their window is a winter wonderland.

"The winds started blowing again a few hours ago. I've never seen such large drifts. I was looking forward to the first Christmas show tonight in the new Lodge," Farmer Bob sighs.

"The families cannot travel to the farm in these horrible conditions. So many children will be disappointed. And the white flakes keep falling." Honey shakes her head in dismay.

"Well, at least the wind gusts stopped. Perhaps the snow plows can clear the roads before tonight."

"Do you think we can still have the show?" Honey asks him hopefully.

"I doubt it. But we will prepare the lodge for the show anyway. The props need to be arranged on the set, and some special lighting needs to be installed."

"Lee Jacque won't be able to finish the mural either," Honey figures.

"I'll scoop as much snow around the truck as I can and load our supplies to take to the lodge," he tells her.

"I will bake the rest of the cookies in the lodge kitchen."

"Good idea. I'll honk the horn when I'm ready for you to come out."

But as soon as the garage door is open the farmer's hope s are dashed. His truck is almost covered in snow, and the road leading to the lodge is filled with knee high drifts. Farmer Bob climbs on his tractor to scoop out a path.

Karibou's heart races with excitement as he makes his own fun. His coat matches the scene and he leaps into asnow drift. His legs sink and he dips his nose in the soft powdery stuff, tossing in up and watching it fall. Snowflake clusters fall from the grey skies.

Karibou races in a circle.

"A perfect day to flop in the pond," he thinks and leaps over a drift on his way there. Three red cardinals take flight to get out of his path. The farm was peaceful and quiet, until Karibou woke up the forest animals with his play. He speeds to the ice covered pond and skids when his paws reach the ice. He glides across, then scrambles, trying to stop himself. The white puppy is spun three times before slowing to a stop. As soon as he regains his footing, he races up to do it again.

Karibou finds the round saucer sled in the garage. As Farmer Bob's tractor puffs gray smoke in the cold air Karibou chooses just the right spot on hill to place the sled. He runs in a circle, kicking up the powdery snow before running full speed and leaping onto the sled. It dashes down the slope and sails over the ice, twirling around and around.

Soon rabbits and squirrels watch the fun-loving puppy. Fenwick comes from his den to see the excitement. A shy fawn peeks from behind a thicket.

"Come on, it's fun-n-n-n-n-n-n-n-n!" Karibou squeals as he sails across the ice. Fenwick joins his friend. When he reaches the pond he too sails across. Soon the rabbits, a beaver and the fawn are all playing on the slippery surface.

The morning passes, and the snow continues to fall. Farmer Bob has trouble and goes back inside.

"We can't use the truck, there is too much snow. The tractor is broken down. We won't be able to get to the Lodge ourselves." Farmer Bob tells Honey as he removes his boots and warm clothing.

"I am so disappointed. The children worked so hard." Honey takes a deep breath. "I'll spread the news. Families will need to know right away."

Farmer Bob pours himself another cup of coffee and warms himself in front of the fire. Karibou's romping catches his attention.

"Come out here, Honey. Would you look at that? We are disappointed by the snow and Karibou is loving it!" When Farmer Bob taps on the window the forest animals scatter. Karibou keeps playing, giving Farmer Bob an idea.

He puts his coat and boots back on. "Don't cancel the show yet!"

Honey bundles up and watches Farmer Bob gets the big sled, called a taboggan, from the garage.

"Karibou, here boy! Karibou!"

As soon as the white dog hears his master's call he races from the pond.

"How would you like to save the day?" he asks the snow dog.

Farmer Bob rigs up a harness and attaches it to the long sled. "Do you think you can pull this, boy? Give it a try."

Karibou knows he can and feels important being asked to help. He easily pulls the sled through the snow and back to Farmer Bob.

"Honey, let's load up the sled. Karibou is going to make this work!" Honey carries the supplies they will need and together they load the sled. Honey piles several quilts on the back. Farmer Bob is careful.

"I will walk alongside, otherwise the load will be too heavy for him." Karibou uses his strong legs and easily pulls the sled toward the lodge.

"He's doing it, he's doing it!" Honey cheers, putting her hands together. Karibou is doing it, but Farmer Bob can't keep up. He struggles behind. Karibou stops, until he catches up.

"Let's go boy!" the farmer huffs. But Karibou doesn't move. He looks at his master and then at the sled.

"You want me to ride? Is that it, boy?" Farmer Bob shakes his head. "That will make the load too heavy. Let's go."

Still Karibou stalls. Farmer Bob thinks for a moment then gently climbs on the back of the sled.

Almost before Farmer Bob is seated Karibou puts his head down and heaves the load. Surprisingly the sled moves with ease. "Karibou is doing it! Karibou you amaze me!" Farmer Bob exclaims, the wind nearly blowing his hat from his head as the snow dog makes his way to the lodge.

After three round trips, all the supplies are delivered.

"What a good job you did Karibou!" they tell him as he shakes the snow from his coat.

Inside, they are delighted to find the mural finished. Ollie the mouse king is startled to see it finished too. He looks around the lodge for Simone.

"It's beautiful. The winter scene she painted as a backdrop to the stage is perfect!" Honey nods and smiles. "The Lodge is different. There is a luster, and a festive feeling."

"It truly is different!" the farmer agrees.

"Oh, here is a note from Lee Jacque."

She reads it aloud.

"Farmer Bob and Honey, I am sorry I didn't get to say goodbye. I hope you like my work. Your Lodge is beautiful. With the weather report so bad, I best be on my way before the winds set in. Until we meet again. Lee Jacque. "

Ollie is stunned by this news. Simone is gone without a goodbye. He walks with slumped shoulders back inside his castle. Once more he feels something he's never felt before, and he doesn't like it. He wishes it would go away.

Ollie's kingdom is preparing to celebrate the holiday, and the elves are now helping to make the mouse houses beautiful. Garland and wreaths, mistletoe and ivy are hung all around and candles decorate every window. From the kitchen of every home aromas from the baking of gingerbread and sugar cookies fill the streets. A group sings Christmas carols.

Cleever rolls a barrel.

"Good afternoon, Your Highness. How are you this fine day?"

Ollie does not want to dampen the spirit of the day. "Never better," he forces a smile.

"Delicious treats are being made for our watch party tonight. We are using this barrel to build a fire pit. Our area will be toasty warm. We are having a gift exchange too. Oh, and Rocky is making his cotton candy bonbons!"

"That sounds like a perfect Christmas Eve." Ollie mutters. "But the weather forecast is not good. If families cannot reach the Lodge, I'm afraid the Christmas Show will be cancelled."

"Let's hope for the best," Cleever tells him.

Ollie walks all the way to his room with his head down, not even noticing the brilliance of the blue stars.

Chapter 15

The fireplace gives a golden glow and the lodge is filled with the sounds, smells and sparkle of Christmas. The farmer and his wife wait as night falls.

"I don't think the snowplows could clear the roads in time. I think we might be the only ones here tonight." Farmer Bob announces.

"We can't control the weather," Honeys sighs.

A knock at the door startles them both. Two angels peer through the window!

"What in the world?" Farmer Bob says, going to the door.

"It's our angels for the show!" Honey cries. The two snow-covered angels are quickly welcomed in.

"We walked up from the road!" they tell the man and wife.

"You made it, I can't believe it! But we may be the only ones here!" Farmer Bob explains.

"Nope, we came with a bus carrying everyone. We got stuck a ways up the road. But I don't think they all can make the walk to the Lodge."

Suddenly Karibou nudges his master. Farmer Bob knows how they can.

"Karibou is a sled dog!" the farmer announces, putting on his winter coat. The giant white Alaskan Malamute proudly goes out into the night. Farmer Bob connects harness again and Karibou pulls families, one by one, to the Lodge. Honey greets each of them at the door with hot cocoa or Christmas Cheer. The children dry their boots and socks near the fire and warm up with Honey's cozy quilts.

When the last family makes it the Lodge is filled with cheers and hoots!

"Merry Christmas everyone. Our show will begin in five minutes." Honey announces.

There is excitement in the air. The children have worked hard. The parents exchange their weather stories, and the wind picks up again.

"What if we get snowed in?" a young child asks her mother.

Honey answers for her.

"We have the warmth of the fireplace, plenty of Christmas treats and lots of quilts," she says.

Chapter 16

The king passes the royal kitchen on his way to watch the first ever Fort Osage Christmas Show. Rocky joins him carrying his tray of yummies.

"You are serving your cotton candy bonbons. Everyone will love that." Ollie says, right before the sound of screams freezes them both. He and Rocky race to the sounds and are met by a mice mob running toward them.

"Run for your lives, run for your lives!" many of them cry as they flee the village square. Ollie struggles to get through the crowd as Hazel flies towards him.

"We've got trouble Ollie, follow me!" The two mice follow the pink ladybug to the village square. Hazel hovers as the mouse king stops dead in his tracks, his mouth dropping open.

The whole village square is filled with spiders! Big spiders and small, but most towering over Ollie. A couple of furry ones rise higher than the buildings. Mice seek safety inside the shops, their frightened faces seen through upper and lower shop windows. Ollie swallows hard. He has never seen this many spiders together before.

Mice who couldn't flee stand behind their king waiting for him to act.

"Colfax?" He tries to sound calm but his voice cracks a little. One large spider from the back makes his way to the front. Many of the spiders shuffle out of his way.

"Is that you Colfax?" he asks with a faked smile. Ollie hopes no one notices his trembling legs.

In a low, scratchy, quiet voice the spider speaks. "It is I, Colfax." Ollie swallows again and scans the army of spiders.

"Is . . . there . . . a . . . problem?" His voice rises on the word problem.

"I only asked one thing, mouse king. To stay away from our webs. And now many of our webs are destroyed." Before the last word is spoken the entire group of spiders shifts a little closer to Ollie. His instincts are to move away, but a king must be brave.

"Oh no, that is terrible news. I am not sure . . ."

Suddenly Cleever pokes the king's shoulder and whispers in his ear. Ollie takes in a deep breath before responding.

"Colfax, in our effort to help the elves get the lodge ready, the trusses and rafters high above were dusted . . ." the tiny mouse swallows a few times before continuing . . . "removing the cobwebs."

With those words the spiders begin marching in place and Ollie's heartbeat quickens. Cleever turns and runs away screaming. Rocky faints and the cotton candy bonbons fall with him. Joleen goes to his side.

Ollie must speak with wisdom and courage, but he does not feel brave. He feels like crying. His cheeks grow hot and

his whole body shakes. Panic bubbles up, almost taking him over. But the words of his mother ring loudly:

"Panic makes you blind to solutions. Do not panic, THINK!"

Ollie refuses to let the fear stop him. He takes a deep breath in and closes his eyes. Then he crosses his arms.

"Hmmmmmm," Ollie pretends he is calm as sweat runs down his face. "May I say something, Colfax?"

The spider replies with a simple word. "Yes."

Ollie clears his throat.

"You are hungry," he says, looking from side to side to address the whole gathering of spiders. "Being hungry is a bad thing. If I can give you food right now, would that help you?" Colfax stares at Ollie, then scans his army.

"You would never have enough food for all of us," Colfax sounds raspy and scary.

"The new Lodge will be a busy place now that the workers are finished. The webs that snagged your meals will be swept away often. We must find a long term answer for your food shortage. Please except our finest fare, cotton candy bonbons. They are delicious, and will fill your hunger for now."

Ollie picks one of the bonbons from the floor and presents it to Colfax. The furry spider sniffs at the strange and colorful confection. He tastes it. With a sticky mouth he replies, "It is good, King Ollie. It is very good."

Ollie picks up more of the bonbons and passes them out to the spiders. All eyes are now off Ollie as they enjoy the yummy treat. Soon other spiders are tearing away portions and sharing them with all.

Ollie goes to Colfax as he munches happily.

"Tonight the bonbons are filling your hunger. But we must find a long term answer to your food shortage. We are happy to share our elderberries and all that we have."

"This food is good. We like bonbons," Colfax's words sound sticky.

"I have a plan," Ollie says. "Could my royal kitchen supply you with cotton candy bonbons a few times a month?"

"Yes," Colfax agrees. "But in the warm months we hunt outside."

Ollie takes note.

"Then in the winter months, my royal kitchen will deliver the bonbons twice each month, and other food if needed. This way we can live as friends, live in harmony. Does that sound good, friend?"

A terrified Rocky brings another tray of the bonbons and Ollie makes sure each spider has his fill.

"Yes, King Ollie. Our hunger is satisfied. We have an agreement. Thank you," Colfax says and leads the spiders out of the village. Ollie takes a deep breath and the mice inside the village square shops escape in relief and follow their king to the watch party.

Chapter 17

The Sparkle Squad has prepared a great space for the watch party. A miniature Christmas tree glistens with mini lights and gold and silver Christmas bulbs. Logs and sticks fill their fire pit, keeping dozens of the mice warm and toasty. Hazel and Karibou, Ollie's mom and Dr. Proctor, the Sparkle Squad, the needle masters and each elf with their teams sit shoulder-to-shoulder.

On the stage below children sing the carols of Christmas, each song filling hearts with warmth. Sugar cookies, gingerbread, ribbon candy, Christmas Cheer Tea, hot cocoa, and candy canes are enjoyed by all. The wind howls outside and lights are low for the final number. Rosy-cheeked children sing the songs of old, and the audience joins in too.

From up high the mice and the elves sing along. Ollie is grateful to have his mother living in the kingdom now and the kind Dr. Proctor to help keep the kingdom healthy.

Before the last song, Hazel hands out song lyrics.

"I rewrote the lyrics just for our kingdom. Please sing along."

When Ollie sings along to the words of the song, he feels the meaning all the way to his toes. The mice lock arms and sway back and forth.

Christmas time is near

Happiness hold dear

Fun for all that mice will call

Their favorite time of the year

Blue stars in the air

Carols everywhere

Older times and ancient rhymes

Our hopes and dreams to share

Snow bells in the air

Beauty everywhere

We'll join by the fireside

And make joyful memories there

Christmas time is dear

We'll be meeting here

Oh, that we could always be

So joyful through the year

Oh, that we could always feel

This beauty the whole year.

When the song is over, the feeling lingers. Jolly takes the crystal from his breast pocket and blue magic stars shoot in all directions, filling every space with a mystical glow.

The sight stumps the elves. Ollie takes the crystal and

examines it before handing it back to Jolly.

"The magic in the crystal was almost gone, how is this possible?" the elf asks. Ollie thinks he knows.

"We all saw the fading blue stars. Jolly sacrificed most of the magic to help build our kingdom. When the lodge needed more magic than what was left, we did what we could to help. We didn't have magic to share, but we had ourselves. Each of you gave a total effort to help the elves make Fort Osage Lodge as special as possible . . . and look at what happened. What a beautiful night this has been! Perhaps the Christmas spirit we feel inside makes its own kind of magic."

The mice agree.

After the gifts are exchanged the party breaks up and they all return to their homes. Ollie goes home too. When he gets there he finds a wrapped gift on his bed.

"For Ollie," it reads. Ollie rips the paper and finds the picture Simone painted of The Nutcracker ballet scene. He reads the card.

I'm sorry I couldn't say goodbye. It was lovely visiting your kingdom. A great king may someday visit Paris? My studio is above the Café de la Paix. Farewell, until meet again.

Simone

Ollie looks at her painting, then reads the note again, his heart soaring.

The mouse king opens a suitcase and begins to pack for an adventure of a lifetime.

Tomorrow when a new day dawns Ollie will begin a new chapter in another real life fairytale at Fort Osage Farm.

About the Author

Author Kim Luke and her husband own, operate and live on a Christmas tree farm. Go to Fortosagefarm.com for seasonal hours of operation and to inquire about seeing the real mouse boot house that Kim writes about. And please like our Fort Osage Farm Facebook page.

Kim also has an adult fantasy series, Circle of Sun. Visit her at www.kimlukeauthor.com, where you will find information about release dates for future books in either series.

If you enjoyed this story, please take a moment to write a review on Amazon so others can enjoy the adventures of Ollie. Please and thank you in advance.

The Enchanted Farm at Fort Osage
TALES OF COURAGE AND ADVENTURE

82820551R00075

Made in the USA
Columbia, SC
06 December 2017